The Magic School Bus

and the Science Fair Expedition

SCIENCE FAIR

WHAT WILL *YOUR* PROJECT BE?

The Magic School Bus

and the Science Fair Expedition

By Joanna Cole

Illustrated by Bruce Degen

Scholastic Press / New York

Many people have helped in the making of this book. Our gratitude goes to John and Mary Gribbin, for their expert review and wonderfully informed perspective. And to Robin Wasserman, for her keen observations. Thanks to John Helms for his expertise — and for weighing the paper clip! To Warren Hirsch and Steven Vizner for astronomy and radium know-how. To Rachel Cole, Heidi Coffin, Mark Goldman, Erica Goldman, and Chris Santoro for their reading and comments. And to Michael Proia on Peaks Island, Maine, for tweaking Arnold's speech bubble on page 28. Appreciation also goes to our editors Kristin Earhart, and especially Craig Walker, who has been inspiring us from the very start. To Stephanie Calmenson for her wise counsel and pertinent questions. And, always, to our spouses Phil Cole and Chris Degen for their enduring support.

Library of Congress Cataloging-in-Publication Data Available

Reinforced Library Edition
ISBN 0-439-90380-7

10 9 8 7 6 5 4 3 2 1   6 7 8 9/0

Printed in Malaysia   46
First edition, August 2006

The text type was set in 15-point Bookman Light.
The illustrator used pen and ink, watercolor, color pencil,
and gouache for the paintings in this book.

To Stephanie Calmenson,
for her generosity, humor, and advice,
but most of all, for her friendship,
which has so enriched my life.
—J.C.

To my dear family,
at home and abroad,
with the world in their hands,
and the earth between their fingers.
—B.D.

In Ms. Frizzle's class, we really needed help!
We were working on projects for the science fair.
The fair was only a few days away,
but some of us had no idea what to do.

6

Then Arnold had a suggestion:
"We could get ideas at the new science museum."
The museum was just around the corner.
We could walk there instead of riding
on our wacky old school bus!

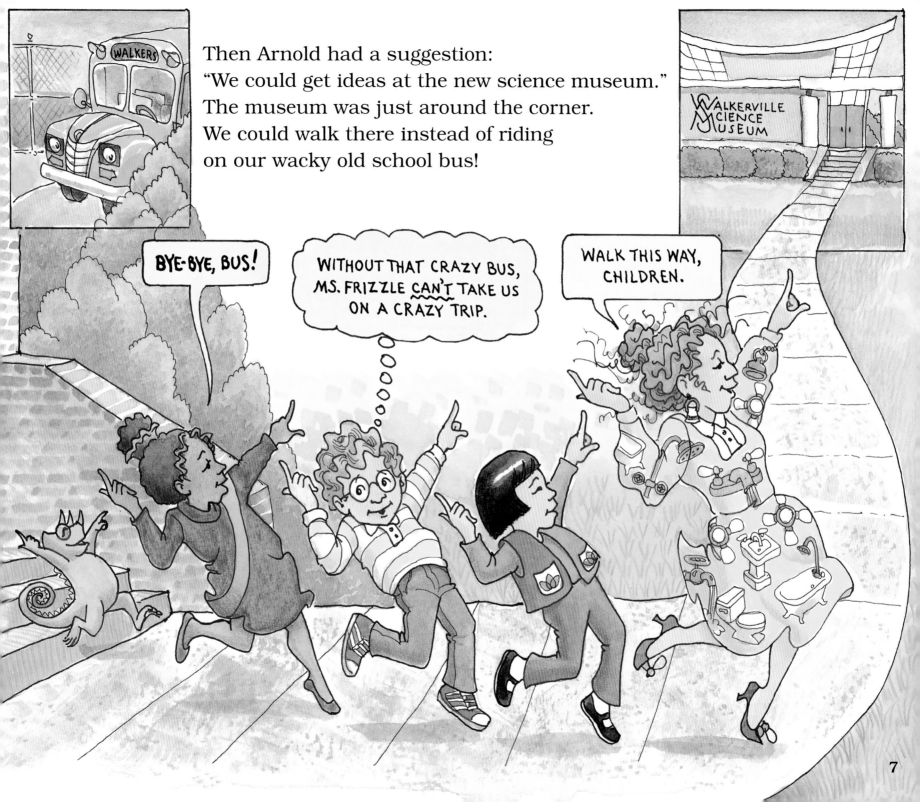

BYE-BYE, BUS!

WITHOUT THAT CRAZY BUS,
MS. FRIZZLE CAN'T TAKE US
ON A CRAZY TRIP.

WALK THIS WAY,
CHILDREN.

WALKERS

WALKERVILLE
SCIENCE
MUSEUM

Then we saw a big cardboard bus.
We could get our picture taken on it.
We all climbed aboard.

10

The photographer snapped the picture.
His flash went off.
Then, wouldn't you know it?
Ms. Frizzle flicked on the high beams.
There was a bigger flash,
and the cardboard bus started moving.

We rolled up to a wide entryway that led to a show on great scientists. "Isn't this wonderful, children?" said Ms. Frizzle. "We're going to learn how scientists work!"

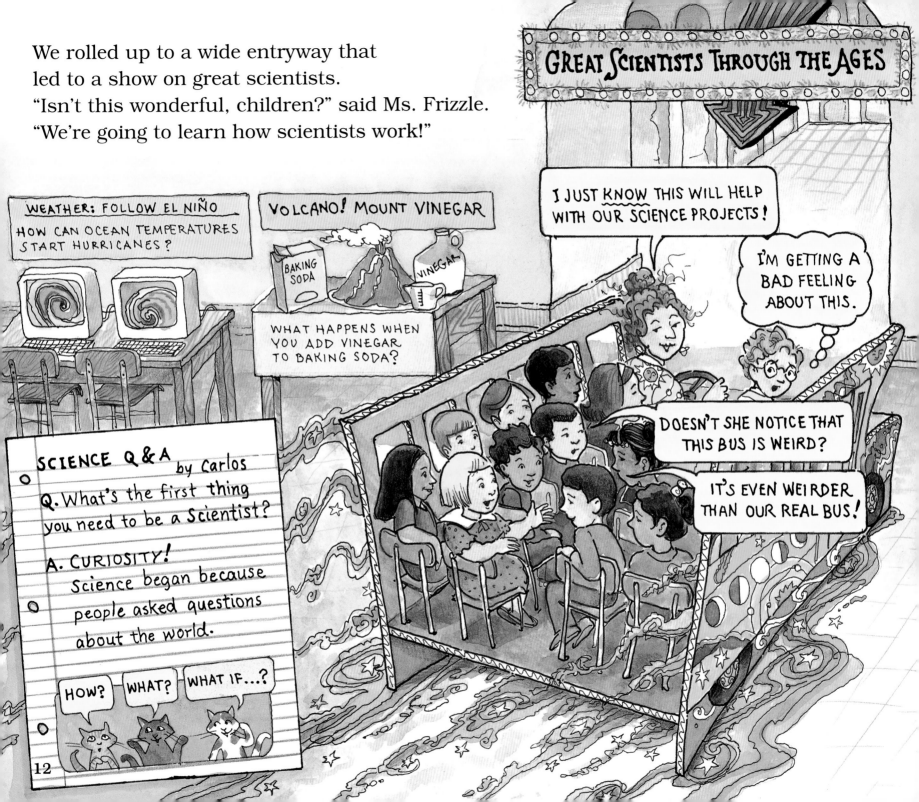

Inside, we saw life-size models
of famous scientists in history.
Our bus glided past a model of Copernicus.
"This famous scientist said that the planets –
including our Earth – went around the sun,"
said Ms. Frizzle.
"But he could not prove it."

EXHIBIT: PART ONE
The Sun and the Planets

COPERNICUS'S
QUESTION:
DOES THE EARTH TRAVEL
AROUND THE SUN?

THE OLD BELIEF:
SUN
EARTH

COPERNICUS'S
BELIEF:
EARTH
SUN

COPERNICUS
Born 1473
Died 1543

IN THE TIME OF COPERNICUS,
MOST PEOPLE THOUGHT THE
EARTH WAS THE CENTER AND
THE SUN WENT AROUND IT.

TODAY WE KNOW
THE SUN
IS AT THE CENTER.

I THOUGHT I WAS THE
CENTER OF EVERYTHING.

WE NOTICED THAT.

As the bus came up to the model of Galileo,
we got a big surprise. The model came to life!
Galileo ran over, knocked on the door, and shouted,
"I'm about to make an important discovery!
I need my telescope! I need a ride home!"

The Friz opened the bus door,
and Galileo hopped on. "You're in luck, Gal,"
said Ms. Frizzle. "We were just leaving."
There was a blinding flash,
and the bus jerked forward.
"Next stop, Italy, four hundred years ago,"
shouted the Friz from the driver's seat.

A STORY ABOUT GALILEO

He Made a Better One

In the early 1600s, people in Italy had never seen a telescope. Then Galileo heard that a man had brought one to his country.

Galileo wanted to look through the telescope, but it was in another part of Italy. So he made one of his own.

Other people had used telescopes to look at ships or armies. Galileo did what no one had done before. He used his to look at the night sky.

The next thing we knew,
the bus had rolled up in front
of a tall, narrow house.
Galileo went in and came out
with a telescope.

16

Almost seventy years had passed since Copernicus's death, but many people still didn't believe his idea that the Earth went around the sun.
"I think Copernicus was right!" said Galileo.

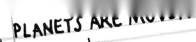

PLANETS ARE MO.....
by Phoebe
People knew that Jupiter and other planets move. For thousands of years they had seen them moving slowly across the sky.

LAST WEEK   TONIGHT

WATCHING VENUS IN THE SKY

Since Galileo's time, more of Jupiter's moons have been seen. Today there are more than sixty!

I have to show that the Earth can move," said Galileo.
That night, he looked at the sky through his telescope.
We got a chance to look, too.
We saw a big planet with four moons around it.
The planet was Jupiter.

I AM THE FIRST PERSON IN THE WORLD TO SEE MOONS GOING AROUND A PLANET!

I'M THE SECOND!   I'M THE THIRD!

I'M GOING TO BE THE 20TH.

Galileo thought hard about his evidence.
Ms. Frizzle told us, "Galileo's discovery was important, class.
It showed that our Earth and moon could move together around the sun."

As we were driving away, we met someone standing in the road and staring into space. It was not the kind of staring into space Galileo did with his telescope. It was the kind that gets you run over by a cardboard bus. The man was Isaac Newton.

MS. FRIZZLE, WATCH OUT FOR THAT MAN!

ISAAC NEWTON, YOU ARE IN THE WRONG TIME AND PLACE.

LET'S TAKE HIM HOME.

SCREECH

Sir Isaac Newton
Born 1642
Died 1727

Newton climbed aboard. Ms. Frizzle flicked on her brights and . . . *FLASH!* The bus took off!

FLASH

In an instant, we were on a farm in England.
Just like that, it was fifty-five years later.
Newton stepped off the bus
and sat under an apple tree.

NEWTON'S QUESTION:
WHAT KEEPS THE PLANETS IN THEIR ORBITS?

HE'S JUST SITTING THERE.

IF HE'S SUCH A BIG SHOT SCIENTIST, SHOULDN'T HE BE DOING AN EXPERIMENT?

DON'T WORRY, CLASS. HE'S THINKING.

SON, DON'T LET THOSE COWS WANDER OFF.

ANOTHER WORD FROM DOROTHY ANN
An orbit is the path of an object- like the Earth- around another object - like the sun.

SUN
EARTH
ORBIT

21

A STORY ABOUT NEWTON

Home from College

In 1665, while Newton was studying at Cambridge University, a terrible disease called the plague broke out.

The university sent all the students home, so they wouldn't get sick. Newton returned to his family farm.

While at home, he discovered many things. The most important was that the laws of motion on Earth are the same laws that control the motion of the whole universe. This idea is called Newton's Law of Universal Gravitation.

Ms. Frizzle said Isaac was thinking about the Earth and the moon.
Thump! Isaac saw an apple fall off the tree.
"Hmm," he said. "I know that the apple was pulled by Earth's gravity.
If gravity's pull can reach to the top of the tree, maybe it can reach as far as the moon."

Now Newton began thinking about the sun and planets. He told us, "The sun's gravity holds the planets and their moons in orbit."

GRAVITY IS THE "GLUE" THAT HOLDS THE UNIVERSE TOGETHER!

NEWTON'S THOUGHTS: (Lots of ideas. No cows.)

SUN

SUN AND PLANETS

HOW GRAVITY MAKES ORBITS
by Keesha

Keesha is like the Earth.
The string is like gravity.
The ball is like the moon.

WHIRL THE BALL (moon) ON THE STRING (gravity).   THEN LET IT GO!

ORBIT

WITHOUT "GRAVITY," THE "MOON" FLIES AWAY.

WE'D BETTER CATCH THOSE COWS.

NEWTON IS SUPPOSED TO BE WATCHING THEM.

HE CAN'T— HE'S THINKING TOO HARD.

23

We thanked Newton and piled into the bus. Ms. Frizzle called from the driver's seat, "Copernicus, Galileo, and Newton studied something very big – the universe! Let's meet scientists who study *small* things." She flicked her brights. In a flash, we were in Holland!

A STORY ABOUT ANTONI VAN LEEUWENHOEK

Looking at Threads

Antoni van Leeuwenhoek was a draper — a seller of cloth. But he was interested in a lot more than cloth. One day he saw a book by an English scientist named Robert Hooke. There were drawings of things Hooke had seen under a microscope. Antoni was amazed.

Antoni knew about magnifiers. Every day he used a magnifying glass to make sure the threads in his cloth were straight and tight. He decided to build his own microscope.

We went into Leeuwenhoek's cloth shop. There he was at the window, peering into an odd little microscope.

LEEUWENHOEK'S MICROSCOPE DOESN'T LOOK LIKE THE ONES WE USUALLY SEE.

HIS HAIRSTYLE DOESN'T LOOK LIKE THE ONES WE USUALLY SEE, EITHER.

IN LEEUWENHOEK'S DAY, MEN WORE WIGS, ARNOLD.

ANTONI VAN LEEUWENHOEK
Born 1632 – Died 1723

"I've spent fifty years looking at things," said Leeuwenhoek. "I'm curious about everything." When he said "everything," he really meant it. It could get kind of gross.

STILL MORE WAYS SCIENTISTS WORK
by Wanda
They use their hands as well as their heads.
(Van Leeuwenhoek worked carefully to build his own microscopes.)

THESE ARE EXCELLENT LENSES, ANTONI.

THANKS, I GRIND THEM MYSELF.

I AM SCRAPING THIS SOFT WHITE STUFF FROM MY TEETH.

LOOK! THERE ARE LITTLE ANIMALS IN IT.

EEUW!

HASN'T HE EVER HEARD OF FLOSSING?

The "little animals" Leeuwenhoek saw in dental plaque were actually bacteria.

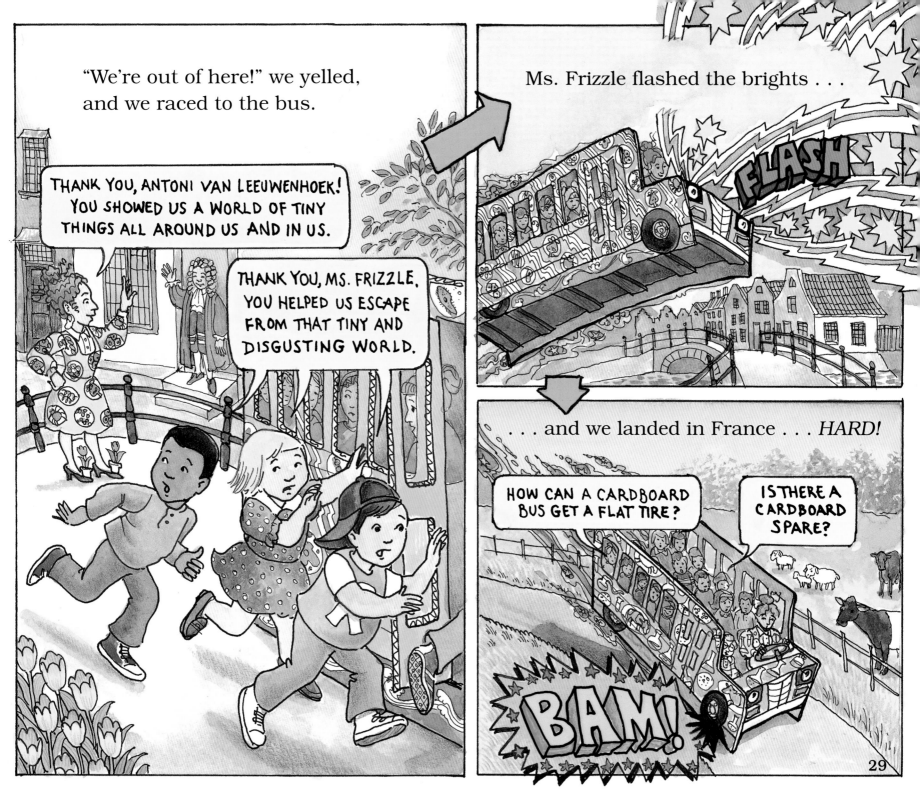

A STORY ABOUT LOUIS PASTEUR

Using Science for Health

Louis grew up in a small French town. He was very good in school, went to the best college in France, and became a scientist.

Soon people began to come to him with problems. Winemakers said, "My wine is going bad." Farmers had sick chickens, cows, and sheep. Louis wanted to help them all.

He began asking questions about all the problems. In his lab he found answers that helped make the world a healthier place.

Suddenly, a distinguished gentleman came by. "May I be of help?" he asked.
"Louis Pasteur!" our teacher answered.
"I was hoping you'd come along."
When the tire was fixed, Louis asked us to drive him home.

We all got on the bus, and Ms. Frizzle
drove us into farm country.
It was beautiful, but many of the farm animals
were sick and dying.
"These animals have a terrible disease called anthrax,"
Pasteur explained. "I am going to work on it.
Please take me to my laboratory in Paris."

PASTEUR'S QUESTION:
WHAT MAKES US SICK?

ABOUT 200 YEARS HAVE PASSED SINCE LEEUWENHOEK FIRST LOOKED AT BACTERIA.

LEEUWENHOEK SAW BACTERIA. BUT HE DIDN'T THINK THEY CAUSED SICKNESS.

I THINK THEY CAN, AND I WANT TO PROVE IT.

TO THE LAB!

CLASS, ISN'T IT WONDERFUL HOW SCIENTIFIC KNOWLEDGE GROWS OVER THE YEARS?

WHAT ARE BACTERIA?
by Shirley

Bacteria are tiny, one-celled living things.
Some cause disease, but most are helpful.

WE CAUSE FOOD POISONING.

WE HELP MAKE CHEESE.

Salmonella enteritidis

Lactobacilli

31

Pasteur carried out a great experiment. It proved that the bacteria caused anthrax. Once he knew that, he was able to make a vaccine that prevented the disease.

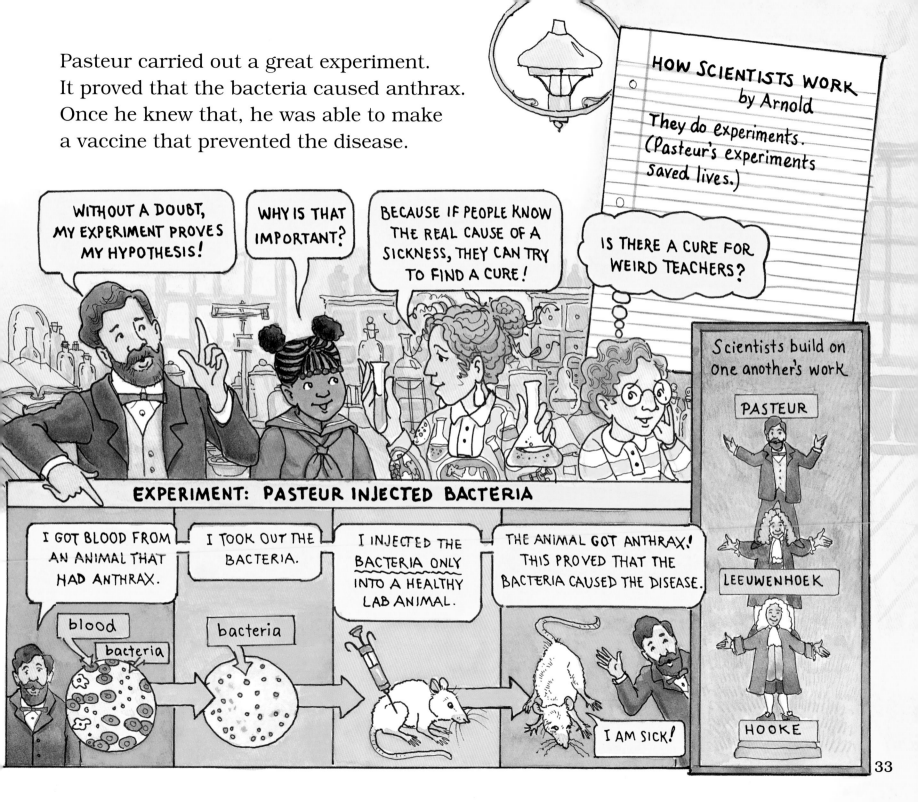

We filed out of Pasteur's lab and onto the bus.
Ms. Frizzle stepped on the gas, flicked on the brights, and — *FLASH!* — the bus went into action.
When it stopped, we were still in Paris, but we were at another laboratory. It was twenty years later.
"Now we'll meet Marie and Pierre Curie," said the Friz.
"They are about to discover something exciting."

WHAT ARE RAYS?
by Florrie
Rays are thin lines of energy.
There are:

light rays, heat rays,

Xrays

and lots of others.

WE'LL WEAR THESE SUITS TO PROTECT US FROM THE DANGEROUS RAYS IN THE CURIES' LAB.

DANGEROUS?

LET'S GO BACK TO THE GUY WHO SCRAPED THE GUNK OFF HIS TEETH!

FLASH

The lab turned out to be a wooden shed. Marie Curie was stirring a big pot over a fire. The stirrer was almost as big as she was! "What's in the pot?" we wondered.

MADAME CURIE, WHY DO YOU WORK IN THIS LEAKY, OLD PLACE?

BECAUSE WOMEN ARE NOT ALLOWED IN THE UNIVERSITY LABS.

WOW, IT MUST HAVE BEEN HARD TO BE A WOMAN SCIENTIST IN THOSE DAYS.

MARIE SKLODOWSKA CURIE
Born 1867~Died 1934

A STORY ABOUT MARIE CURIE

How She Got to Paris

Marie Curie was a famous scientist who worked in Paris, France. She came there from Poland, and her original name was Marya Sklodowska. Marya loved to learn. But at that time in Poland, girls were not allowed to go to college.

She worked for six years and saved enough money to go to the University of Paris. She was still so poor that she lived in an attic and ate almost nothing but tea and bread.

Marya changed her name to a French name, Marie. Later, when she married Pierre Curie, she changed her last name, too.

WHAT MAKES SOME
MATERIALS
GIVE OFF RAYS?

WHAT IS RADIOACTIVITY?
by Amanda Jane

Some materials are radioactive.
That means they give off
invisible rays.

When Marie Curie started her
work, no one knew what the
rays were made of.

I AM ANTOINE HENRI BECQUEREL.
IN 1896, I FOUND URANIUM IN
PITCHBLENDE. IT WAS THE FIRST
RADIOACTIVE ELEMENT TO BE
DISCOVERED. MARIE CURIE
WANTED TO FIND MORE.

Wanda looked in the pot. "It's just mud," she said.
"This stuff is called pitchblende," said Marie.
"I am trying to find a radioactive material in it."

I DON'T REALLY
UNDERSTAND
RADIOACTIVITY.

JUST WAIT AND
WE'LL LEARN ALL
ABOUT IT!

WE ALWAYS DO
IN MS. FRIZZLE'S
CLASS.

Marie's husband, Pierre, was a scientist, too.
He became so interested in Marie's research that
he gave up his own work and started helping her.
Marie and Pierre Curie found a way to take
the radioactive matter out of the pitchblende.

WHAT THE CURIES DID
by Phoebe
1. Shoveled pitchblende.
2. Boiled the pitchblende and let it cool.
3. Skimmed crystals off the top.
4. Tested them for radioactivity.
5. Saved only the radioactive crystals.
6. Started all over again.

WE FOUND AN ELEMENT THAT WAS A MILLION TIMES MORE RADIOACTIVE THAN URANIUM.

I NAMED IT RADIUM.

IF I FOUND A NEW ELEMENT, I'D NAME IT JIM.

PIERRE CURIE
Born 1859 - Died 1906

AGAIN?

...AND OVER AND OVER AND OVER AGAIN!

IT TOOK THREE YEARS

The Curies had to work long and hard.

IRON ROD

CAST-IRON POT

They used seven tons of pitchblende.

1 2 3 4 5 6 7

They were able to get only $\frac{1}{10}$ gram of radium.

$\frac{1}{10}$ gram radium

Even a paper clip weighs more than that.

$\frac{3}{10}$ gram

They found just a little bit of radium, but it helped Marie make a big discovery. "Marie realized that radioactivity must come from inside the radium," said Pierre. "Radium must be spitting out super-tiny parts of its atoms," said Marie. "When the atomic particles come out, energy comes out, too."

WHAT ARE ATOMS?
by John
Atoms are tiny, tiny bits. They are too small to see even with a microscope. Everything is made of atoms, even people.

MY ATOMS JUST LOVE HELIUM ATOMS.

HELIUM BALLOON

HOW WE USE RADIOACTIVE MATERIALS
by Amanda Jane
Radium gives off some of its energy as heat. Pierre Curie found that he could use this heat to make water boil. There are many other uses for radioactivity.

SOME USES ARE HELPFUL TO PEOPLE.

OTHERS ARE HARMFUL.

NUCLEAR MEDICINE

NUCLEAR WEAPONS

A SIMPLE ATOM: HELIUM ATOM

NUCLEUS (CENTER)

THERE'S ENERGY IN ATOMS!

IT'S ATOMIC ENERGY!

RADIUM GIVES OFF HEAT ENERGY AND LIGHT ENERGY.

WE LOVE TO VISIT THE LAB AT NIGHT.

IT GIVES OFF A BEAUTIFUL BLUE LIGHT.

PIERRE'S EXPERIMENT
A bit of radium in a beaker of water will make the water boil.

Today we know that too much
radioactivity is harmful.
But the Curies didn't know that.
Dorothy Ann read from her book:
"They didn't protect themselves.
After a while, they became very sick."

A MORE COMPLEX ATOM: RADIUM

RADIOACTIVITY:
nucleus of radium atom
spits out pieces

OUR SUITS ARE PROTECTING US.

I WISH WE COULD WARN THE CURIES.

BUT MS. FRIZZLE TOLD US THERE IS NO WAY TO CHANGE THE PAST.

CLASS, LET'S THANK THE CURIES AND BE ON OUR WAY.

DANGEROUS NOTEBOOKS
by Tim

Even today, the Curies'
notebooks are so radioactive
that they are kept in
radiation-proof containers.

HOW SCIENTISTS WORK
by Arnold

They put in long hours.
(The Curies worked night
and day for years to
discover radium.)

Sometimes scientists take
risks, whether they
mean to or not.
(The Curies did not know
their work was dangerous.)

A STORY ABOUT ALBERT EINSTEIN

A Compass to Play With

One day, when Albert was about five years old, he was sick in bed. His father gave him a compass to play with.

Albert moved the compass all around, but the needle always kept pointing north. He realized that an invisible force was acting on the needle.

Einstein's life's work was to find out about the hidden forces of the universe.

We waved good-bye and went outside.
A passenger was sitting quietly
at the very back of the cardboard bus.
It was Albert Einstein,
the most famous scientist ever!

Then Ms. Frizzle flashed the lights, and the bus took off! As we traveled, Einstein told us about his work. "Most people have heard of my famous mathematical formula, $E = mc^2$," he said. "But many don't know what it means."

$E = mc^2$ EXPLAINS THAT MATTER AND ENERGY ARE REALLY FORMS OF THE SAME THING.

"MATTER CAN CHANGE TO ENERGY, AND ENERGY CAN CHANGE TO MATTER".

THAT'S WHAT HAPPENED IN THE CURIES' LAB!

YES, RADIUM—WHICH IS MATTER—CHANGED INTO HEAT AND LIGHT—WHICH ARE ENERGY!

A LAST WORD FROM DOROTHY ANN

Matter is all of the stuff in the universe, such as plants, pencils, pennies, and cats.

WHAT $E = mc^2$ DOES
by Phil

* It tells how the sun makes heat and light.
* It explains radioactivity.
* It tells how the universe began.

DID YOU KNOW?

IF THE MASS OF 100 PENNIES WERE CHANGED TO PURE ENERGY, IT COULD POWER NEW YORK STATE FOR TWO DAYS.

SCIENTISTS JUST DON'T KNOW HOW TO DO THAT YET.

ONE CENT

ONE CENT

The bus zoomed to the science museum,
bumped up the steps, rolled through the doors,
and stopped at Einstein's spot in the exhibit.
He stepped into place just in time.
No one had missed him yet.

Einstein said,
"The important thing is
never to stop questioning."

OUR CLASS WILL UNDERSTAND YOUR IDEAS WHEN THEY ARE OLDER, ALBERT.

MUCH OLDER!

TAKE YOUR TIME. IT TOOK ME A WHILE TO UNDERSTAND THEM MYSELF!

EVEN MS. FRIZZLE CAN'T EXPLAIN EINSTEIN TO US.

EVEN EINSTEIN CAN'T EXPLAIN YOUR BUS TO ME!

EINSTEIN'S IDEAS CHANGED HOW WE SEE THE UNIVERSE
by Phoebe

Einstein had many amazing ideas — not just $E=mc^2$.
Many of them seem impossible, but they have been proved by experiments and math.
His work inspired other scientists to ask new questions.

What is SPACE-TIME?

What is RELATIVITY?

what is the FABRIC of the UNIVERSE?

WHAT IS FOR LUNCH?

ALBERT EINSTEIN
Born 1879
Died 1955

GUARD

42

Then our teacher drove over to the photographer. Our picture was ready. It was amazing. Everyone was in it — even the scientists! It must have been magic.

Back at school, everyone got busy.
We all had great questions to ask, such as:
"How do you make a compass?"
"How do plants get water?"
and "What pattern will be on
Ms. Frizzle's dress tomorrow?"

45

the Gallery of Scientists

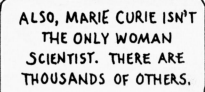

ALSO, MARIE CURIE ISN'T THE ONLY WOMAN SCIENTIST. THERE ARE THOUSANDS OF OTHERS.

GENETICS

BARBARA McCLINTOCK

SO FAR, AT LEAST TWELVE NOBEL PRIZES HAVE BEEN AWARDED TO WOMEN IN SCIENCE.

RADIOACTIVITY

IRÈNE JOLIOT-CURIE

THE IMPORTANT THING IS THAT YOU TOLD US HOW SCIENTISTS THINK...

SPLITTING THE ATOM

LISE MEITNER

...AND HOW SCIENTISTS BUILD ON ONE ANOTHER'S IDEAS...

ELECTROMAGNETISM

MICHAEL FARADAY

...AND THAT SCIENCE IS ALWAYS OPEN TO NEW DISCOVERIES.

ORIGIN OF SPECIES

CHARLES DARWIN

YES, I THINK THEY DID A GOOD JOB.

PHYSICS

ALBERT EINSTEIN

THANK YOU.

WE TRIED.

IT WAS GREAT MEETING YOU.